ONE MORE HUG

By Megan Alexander
Illustrated by Hiroe Nakata

ALADDIN New York London Toronto Sydney New Delhi

One night at bedtime you put on your superhero pajamas, and I tucked you in.

Then a branch tapped on your window, and you called,

"One more hug, Mama."

One day you slayed a leaf dragon
with a make-believe sword,
and I kissed your cheek.

Then your sword broke in two, and you cried,
"One more kiss, Mama."

One morning you waited for the school bus
with your monster backpack,

and I squeezed you tight.

Then the bus doors opened with a loud SCREEEEECH,
and you whispered,
"One more squeeze, Mama."

And I waved as the bus drove away
down, down, down the street,
and you waved back.

And the years flew by,

and you grew bigger

and wiser

and stronger.

And before long, you outgrew your superhero pajamas,

and you climbed the tree outside
your bedroom window.

And before long, you put away your
make-believe sword,
and you rode your bike without any help.

And before long, you left
your monster backpack in
the closet,
and you raced to the bus stop
with your friends.

But even though you were older, you were still my boy.
And you asked for . . .

one more hug
before your big
performance.

One more kiss after you slipped on the ice.

One more song before bedtime.

And the years flew by,

and you grew bigger

and wiser

and stronger.

And before long, you stopped climbing the tree
outside your window,
and learned how to climb a rock wall,
and taught your little brother how to ride your bike,

and joined the track team,
and ran all the way to school.

Until one day I waved as you drove away
down, down, down the street,
and you waved back.

And I closed my eyes and wondered
if you knew how proud you made me,
if you knew how much I loved you,
if you knew you were still my boy, now and forever,
and if you knew that I would always be here for you.

But then you surprised me.

And you wrapped your arms
around me and asked for . . .

one
more
hug.

Photo by Nick Coleman Photography

THE STORY BEHIND THE STORY

OH, HOW LIFE CHANGED WHEN I WAS

blessed with two sons—first Chace, and then four years later, Catcher. Suddenly I was looking at the world through their sweet eyes and experiencing their emotions.

When Chace was five years old and boarding the school bus for kindergarten for the first time, the moment he spotted the bus coming down the street, he felt anxious. As he saw it turn the corner and slowly approach our stop, he looked up at me and asked for a hug. Then he asked for another, and another, always whispering, "One more hug, Mama!" As he got in line to step onto the bus, he ran back to me, leapt into my arms, and asked for "one more hug." We probably exchanged five or six hugs before he finally got on the bus.

At nighttime when his father and I tucked him into bed, we would kiss and hug him and say our prayers, and as we slowly walked to his door, inevitably he would call out for "one more hug!" "There is always time for one more hug," we would answer, and walk back toward his bed.

This idea of needing reassurance or asking for comfort has really touched my heart and soul. According to Child Trends, a leading nonprofit research organization in the US, children receive lifelong positive outcomes when their parents express warmth and affection to them.

With this book, I hope I can help parents like me ponder and reflect on how important it is to encourage all our children to share their feelings. When they ask for one more hug, consider how important this request is. It is more than just a hug—our children are asking for comfort, expressing their feelings, and explaining what they need. How we respond in those moments will have a lasting impact on their lives.

As boys get older, society tends to send the message that they need to hide their feelings and "shake it off." Is this always helpful? Don't we always need to share our emotions, and ask for and receive comfort, for the rest of our lives? Perhaps continuing to encourage the expression of feelings will help the overall well-being and emotional health of this next generation of young men.

One More Hug is the sweet story of my journey with my older son, Chace, now age eight. And

CONTINUED ON NEXT PAGE

Catcher, his younger brother, now age four, is starting to ask for the same request. They both repeat the sweet yet important words: "Stay with me, Mama. One more hug. One more kiss." And what started as a simple request is turning into an important promise from their parents: that comfort will always be available, and no request is ever silly, no matter how old you get.

This book also inspired me to write an original song titled "One More." I wrote this children's lullaby in Nashville with my fellow songwriters, Michael Ochs and Lucas Hoge. Playing the guitar for my boys is part of our bedtime routine, and it is my hope that this sweet lullaby will bless you and your family and help us all cherish each moment in life. You can listen to the song by downloading the link found on the back cover or going to www.MeganAlexander.com.

To Chace

As my firstborn son, you were the first to call out "One more hug,
Mama." This book came to life because of your simple request.
What a gift that was and is. Thank you for being you.

To Catcher

I love you to the moon and back, and you are always my baby boy!
You are gentle, strong, brave, and carefree—never forget it!

Your father and I love you both so much! You are the greatest gifts God
could give. Keep dreaming big dreams. You both make me so proud.
I promise you—we will always have time for one more.

May this book encourage families everywhere to always make time for one more.

—M. A.

To Koharu and Kei —H. N.

ALADDIN / An imprint of Simon & Schuster Children's Publishing Division / 1230 Avenue of the Americas, New York, New York 10020 / First Aladdin hardcover edition November 2019 / Text copyright © 2019 by Megan Alexander / Illustrations copyright © 2019 by Hiroe Nakata / Watercolor stripes copyright © 2019 by istock.com/olga_z / All rights reserved, including the right of reproduction in whole or in part in any form. / ALADDIN and related logo are registered trademarks of Simon & Schuster, Inc. / For information about special discounts for bulk purchases, please contact Simon & Schuster Special Sales at 1-866-506-1949 or business@simonandschuster.com. / The Simon & Schuster Speakers Bureau can bring authors to your live event. For more information or to book an event contact the Simon & Schuster Speakers Bureau at 1-866-248-3049 or visit our website at www.simonspeakers.com. / Book designed by Karin Paprocki / The illustrations for this book were rendered in watercolor and ink. / The text of this book was set in Adobe Fangsong Std. / Manufactured in China 0819 SCP / 2 4 6 8 10 9 7 5 3 1 / Library of Congress Control Number 2019931559 / ISBN 978-1-5344-2971-0 (hc) / ISBN 978-1-5344-2972-7 (eBook)